·LIONEL·
IN THE SUMMER

·LIONEL· IN THE SUMMER

by Stephen Krensky
pictures by Susanna Natti

PUFFIN BOOKS

For Laura
S.K.

For Sirkka and Elias
S.N.

PUFFIN BOOKS
Published by the Penguin Group
Penguin Putnam Books for Young Readers, 345 Hudson Street, New York, New York 10014, U.S.A.
Penguin Books Ltd, 27 Wrights Lane, London W8 5TZ, England
Penguin Books Australia Ltd, Ringwood, Victoria, Australia
Penguin Books Canada Ltd, 10 Alcorn Avenue, Toronto, Ontario, Canada M4V 3B2
Penguin Books (N.Z.) Ltd, 182-190 Wairau Road, Auckland 10, New Zealand

Penguin Books Ltd, Registered Offices: Harmondsworth, Middlesex, England

First published in the United States of America by Dial Books for Young Readers,
a member of Penguin Putnam Inc., 1998
Published by Puffin Books, a member of Penguin Putnam Books for Young Readers, 2000

9 10 8

THE LIBRARY OF CONGRESS HAS CATALOGED THE DIAL EDITION AS FOLLOWS:
Krensky, Stephen.
Lionel in the summer/by Stephen Krensky;
pictures by Susanna Natti.—1st ed.
p. cm.
Summary: Lionel enjoys the longest day of summer, celebrates the Fourth of July, has a lemonade
stand, and travels on vacation with his family.
ISBN 0-8037-2243-5 (trade).—ISBN 0-8037-2244-3 (lib. bdg.)
[1. Summer—Fiction.] I. Natti, Susanna, ill. II. Title.
PZ7.K883Lle 1998 [E]—dc21 97-10218 CIP AC

Puffin Easy-to-Read ISBN 978-0-14-130824-1
Puffin® and Easy-to-Read® are registered trademarks of Penguin Putnam Inc.

Printed in the United States of America

The full-color artwork was prepared using pencil, colored pencils, and watercolor washes.

Reading Level 2.1

CONTENTS

THE LONGEST DAY

On the first day of summer

Lionel woke up early.

He raced cars around a track.

They were going at top speed.

"Lionel!" Father called out.

"Shut off those engines."

Earth is getting very crowded,

thought Lionel.

So he took his spaceship

and flew to another galaxy.

Lionel explored three planets

before his spaceship was attacked.

"Red alert!" shouted Lionel.

"Abandon ship!"

"Lionel!" Mother called out.

"If you're going to make all that noise,

go outside."

Lionel ate a quick breakfast

and went into the backyard.

First he made a castle

out of sticks and stones.

Then he dug a moat to protect the castle

from wild animals.

He was just filling it with water

when his friend Jeffrey arrived.

"Your mother says

you've been up for hours,"

said Jeffrey.

"Are you sick?"

"No," said Lionel.

"Did Louise wake you up?"

Jeffrey asked.

Lionel laughed.

"You know Louise never gets up

if she doesn't have to."

"Then why were you up so early?"

Jeffrey asked.

"I couldn't help it," said Lionel.

"I have too much to do."

"Summer is just starting,"

said Jeffrey.

"Why are you so busy?"

"This is the longest day of the year,"

said Lionel.

"Other days always run out

before I'm finished with them.

But not today."

He unfolded a piece of paper

from his pocket.

"I made this big list of things to do.

Today's my best chance

to fit everything in."

"But, Lionel," said Jeffrey,

"the longest day doesn't have any

more hours in it. It's just the day

when the sun stays out the longest."

Lionel frowned.

"You mean I don't really have extra time?" he asked.

"Sorry," said Jeffrey.

Lionel stopped to think.

"All right," he said, "then I'm going straight to the bottom of the list. I was saving the best for last."

"What's that?" asked Jeffrey.

"Exploring in the woods?

Spying on Louise?"

Lionel shook his head.

"Doing nothing," he said.

"It's the best part of any summer day."

"Sounds good to me," said Jeffrey.

And they lay in the hammock

till lunch.

FIREWORKS

Lionel was very excited.

His whole family was going

to the Fourth of July carnival.

"This is an important holiday,"

said Father.

"The time when we celebrate

our country's birthday."

"Why do we have fireworks?"

asked Louise.

"The country is so big,"

said Mother,

"birthday candles aren't enough."

Lionel smiled.

"I love fireworks," he said.

"How can you be so sure?" said Louise.

"You always fall asleep

before they start."

"Not this year," said Lionel.

"I was little before. Now I'm big."

Louise snorted.

"We'll see," she said.

The carnival was filled with

bright lights and loud noises.

Lionel went on the roller coaster first.

It went up and down

and up again.

Lionel yelled on the ups,

and he yelled on the downs too.

"Wide awake!" he shouted to Louise.

They went on the Ferris wheel next.

It went around and around.

"You're starting to look a little tired,"

said Louise.

Lionel frowned.

He tried to sit up straight.

When the ride was over,

they each got a treat.

Louise had cotton candy.

Lionel ate a caramel apple.

It felt heavy in his hand.

He blinked a few times.

Louise laughed.

"It won't be long now," she said.

Lionel yawned.

He had to do something soon

or it would be too late.

He looked around for an idea.

"Let's go in the Haunted House,"

he said.

Louise was surprised.

"But, Lionel," she reminded him,

"you hate haunted houses.

There are ghosts

and other creepy things inside."

Lionel nodded.

He was counting on that.

"Okay," said Louise. "Let's go."

Father and Mother waited at the exit.

"Aiieeee!"

"Did you hear that scream?" asked Father.

"It sounded like Lionel."

"Oooooooooohhh!"

"Did you hear that groan?" asked Mother.

"It sounded like Lionel too."

A minute later

Lionel and Louise came out.

Louise was laughing.

Lionel was not.

He was frightened and scared.

But at least he wasn't sleepy.

His eyes were wide open.

When the fireworks started,

Lionel watched the colors explode

against the sky.

It was like magic.

"Happy birthday!" he shouted

after each flash and boom.

And he didn't fall asleep

until it was time to go home.

THE LEMONADE STAND

Lionel was busy on his front lawn.

He set up a table and a sign.

Then he brought out

paper cups and a pitcher of lemonade.

He was ready for business.

"What are you doing, Lionel?"

asked Louise.

"I am selling lemonade," said Lionel.

"Everyone will buy some.

Then I'll be rich."

Louise laughed.

"There's a bug in the pitcher,"

she said.

Lionel took it out.

"No free samples," he told the bug.

Louise shook her head.

"Nobody will stop here, Lionel,"

she said.

"There isn't enough traffic,

and your sign is too small.

Besides, you're just a little kid."

Lionel shrugged. "We'll see," he said.

Louise laughed again and left.

Lionel sat and waited.

One car passed.

But it didn't stop.

Lionel sighed.

It was very hot sitting in the sun.

He was getting thirsty.

So he poured himself

a cup of lemonade.

But just to be fair,

he took out a quarter

and paid for it.

Lionel waited some more.

It was still hot.

So he bought himself another drink.

Two more cars passed.

Lionel bought two more drinks.

Soon Louise came back.

"So, Lionel," she asked,

"are you rich yet?"

Lionel looked in his box.

"I have four quarters," he said.

Louise was impressed.

"A dollar already! That's amazing."

She paused.

"Can I sell lemonade too?"

Lionel wiped his forehead.

He was tired of sitting in the sun.

"I'll give you the rest

for a dollar," he said.

"Then you can have your own business."

Louise looked at the pitcher.

There was a lot of lemonade left in it.

She would be rich if she sold it all.

"All right," she said.

"It's a deal."

Louise paid Lionel a dollar

and took his seat behind the table.

"You know, Lionel," she said,

"you'll never get rich

giving up so easily."

Lionel smiled.

"I know," he said,

"but I'm just a little kid, Louise."

Then he went off to play.

THE CAR TRIP

Lionel and his family

were on vacation.

They were seeing the sights.

"This is the life," said Father.

Mother nodded.

"No phone calls or faxes," she said.

"Just peace and quiet."

"Stop poking me, Louise,"

said Lionel.

"I wasn't poking," said Louise.

"You just got in the way

of my finger."

"That's because you're on my side

of the seat," said Lionel.

"Prove it!" said Louise.

"That's enough," said Father.

"Both of you are missing the view.

Just look at that sky."

Lionel looked. Louise looked too.

It was sky all right.

"What do those clouds

make you think of?" asked Father.

"Ice cream," said Lionel.

"Vanilla ice cream

that's melted a little."

"Yes, yes," said Father.

"They do, I guess."

They drove a little more.

"Look at that mountain!"

said Mother.

Lionel looked. Louise looked too.

It was a mountain, all right.

"You don't see a mountain like that

every day," said Mother.

"What does it make you think of?"

"An ice cream cone," said Louise.

"The big waffle kind.

Upside down, of course."

"I hadn't thought of that," Mother admitted.

"I suppose it does."

They drove a little more.

"Wow!" said Father.

"What an amazing river!"

Lionel looked. Louise looked too.

It was a river all right.

"We don't have rivers like that

at home," said Father.

"We sure don't," said Mother.

Lionel and Louise

noticed the mud near the shore.

"It makes me think

of chocolate sauce," said Lionel.

"For once I agree with you,"

said Louise.

"I wonder what else we can see."

Lionel pointed to some waves.

A red buoy bobbed above them.

"Don't forget the whipped cream,"

he said, "with a cherry on top."

"And look!" cried Louise,

spotting some wildflowers.

"Sprinkles too."

Lionel nodded.

They both sighed.

Father and Mother

looked at each other.

"All right, all right," said Father.

"We get the message," said Mother.

They pulled up

to the next ice cream stand.

Lionel and Louise smiled.

It was the best sight

they had seen all day.